ECLIPSE REALMS:

LUNAR SHADOWS

LUNA ARWEN

To my sister, Elizabeth,

Wherever you are, may this book carry the whispers of our shared dreams and the echoes of our laughter. Your spirit, love, and endless support have been my guiding light, even across the distances that separate us. This journey would not have been possible without you.

In every moonbeam, I find a piece of your strength. In every shadow, I sense your unwavering presence. This story is as much yours as it is mine—a testament to our bond and the magic you brought into my life.

Forever and always,

Luna

CONTENTS

PROLOGUE

The moon hung high in the night sky, casting its silvery glow over the quiet town of Crescent Grove. Beneath its ethereal light, shadows danced and shifted, whispering ancient secrets to those who dared to listen. On nights like these, the line between the mundane and the mystical blurred, and long-forgotten powers stirred from their slumber.

Deep within the forest that bordered the town, a circle of ancient stones stood as silent sentinels, remnants of an age long past. In the center of the circle, a figure cloaked in midnight blue knelt, murmuring an incantation that had been passed down through generations. Her voice, barely a whisper, carried on the breeze, mingling with the rustling leaves and the distant hoot of an owl.

The woman's eyes, as dark as the night itself,

glowed with an inner light as she raised her hands toward the moon. "By the light of the moon and the power of the stars, awaken, O' Guardian, and take your place among us."

As she spoke, the air around her shimmered, and a soft, ethereal light enveloped the stones. Slowly, almost imperceptibly, a figure began to materialize within the circle, its form coalescing from the very essence of the night. The woman smiled, her heart swelling with pride and reverence. The Guardian had been awakened, and with it, a new chapter in the ancient struggle between light and dark had begun.

Little did anyone in Crescent Grove know, this awakening would soon touch the life of an unsuspecting girl, setting her on a path that would change her destiny forever.

Chapter 1

AWAKENING

Amara Matthews had always considered herself an ordinary girl. At sixteen, her life revolved around the usual teenage concerns: school, friends, and the occasional bout of high school drama. She lived in a modest house on Elm Street with her mother, Claire, a nurse who worked long hours at the local hospital. Her father had passed away when she was just a baby, leaving behind little more than a few photographs and a legacy she barely understood.

On the night of her sixteenth birthday, Amara sat on her bed, flipping through an old photo album. The pictures were a mix of her childhood memories and faded images of her father. She lingered on a photo of him standing beside her mother, both of them smiling brightly. Her father's eyes seemed to hold a secret, a depth she couldn't quite grasp.

A soft knock on her door pulled her from her reverie. Her mother entered the room carrying a small, intricately carved wooden box. "Happy Birthday, sweetheart," she said, placing the box on the bed beside Amara. "This belonged to your father. He wanted you to have it when you turned sixteen."

Amara traced her fingers over the delicate carvings, a mix of celestial symbols and intricate patterns. "What is it?" she asked, her curiosity piqued.

"It's a family heirloom," Claire explained, her voice tinged with a hint of nostalgia. "Your father's family has always been… special. Open it."

With a sense of anticipation, Amara lifted the lid. Inside, nestled in a bed of velvet, was a pendant shaped like a crescent moon, adorned with tiny, glimmering gemstones. As her fingers brushed against it, a strange sensation washed over her, a warmth spreading from her fingertips to her core.

Suddenly, the room seemed to shimmer, and Amara felt a rush of energy. Her vision blurred, and she saw flashes of another world – a world bathed in moonlight, where shadows moved with a life of their own. She heard whispers, ancient and powerful, calling her name.

"Amara… Guardian…"

Gasping, she dropped the pendant, and the vision faded. She looked up at her mother, who watched her with a mixture of concern and understanding. "What… what just happened?"

Claire took a deep breath, her expression serious. "There's something I need to tell you, Amara. Something about your father, and about who you really are."

Chapter 2

THE MOON GUARDIAN LEGACY

Amara's head spun with the weight of her mother's words. "A Moon Guardian? Me?" she asked, barely able to process the information.

Claire nodded, her eyes filled with both worry and pride. "Yes, Amara. Your father was a Moon Guardian, and now, it's your turn to carry on the legacy. The pendant you touched has awakened your powers."

Amara looked down at the pendant, now resting in her hand. It seemed to pulse with a gentle, comforting warmth. "But... I don't know anything about being a Guardian. How am I supposed to protect anything?"

Claire placed a reassuring hand on her shoulder.

"You won't be alone. There are others like you, and they will help you learn and grow. For now, you need to rest. Tomorrow, I'll take you to someone who can explain everything."

Sleep eluded Amara that night. Her mind buzzed with questions and a nervous excitement. When morning finally came, she dressed quickly and found her mother waiting by the door, car keys in hand.

They drove to the edge of town, towards the forest. Amara had always found the woods a little eerie, but today, they seemed different. There was a sense of anticipation in the air, as if the trees themselves were whispering secrets.

Claire parked the car, and they walked a short distance to a small, hidden clearing. In the center stood an old, weathered cottage. "This is where you'll meet the Council of Guardians," Claire explained. "They've been expecting you."

Amara's heart pounded as they approached the door. Claire knocked, and a moment later, it creaked open to reveal an elderly woman with sharp, piercing eyes. "Claire, it's good to see you again," she said warmly. Her gaze shifted to Amara. "And you must be Amara. We've been waiting for you."

The woman introduced herself as Selene, the head of the Moon Guardians. She led them inside, where a group of people of various ages and backgrounds were gathered. Each of them wore the crescent moon pendant around their necks.

"Welcome, Amara," Selene said, guiding her to a seat. "Your journey as a Guardian begins today. You will learn about our history, our purpose, and most importantly, your own powers."

Over the next few hours, Amara was introduced to the world of the Moon Guardians. She learned that they were part of an ancient order, tasked with maintaining the balance between light and dark forces. They drew their power from the moon, using its energy to protect the world from shadowy threats.

Amara was fascinated but also overwhelmed. It was a lot to take in. Selene sensed her apprehension and placed a comforting hand on her shoulder. "Remember, Amara, you are not alone. We are a family, and we will guide you every step of the way."

As the day turned to evening, Amara felt a mix of emotions. She was excited about her newfound abilities but also nervous about the responsibilities that came with them. She knew her life would never be the same, but she was ready to embrace her destiny.

That night, as she lay in bed, Amara clutched the pendant tightly. She felt a connection to her father, to the legacy he had passed on to her. And for the first time, she felt a sense of purpose, a calling that resonated deep within her soul.

Chapter 3

A NEW WORLD

The next morning, Amara awoke with a renewed sense of determination. She was eager to learn more about her powers and the world she was now a part of. Her mother drove her back to the cottage, where Selene and the other Guardians were waiting.

"Today, we will begin your training," Selene announced. "Your powers are still raw, but with practice, you will learn to control and harness them."

Amara was introduced to her mentor, a young Guardian named Lucas. He was a few years older than her, with a confident demeanor and a friendly smile. "Welcome to the team, Amara," he said, shaking her hand. "Let's get started."

They moved to a clearing behind the cottage,

where Lucas began teaching Amara the basics of her abilities. "The moon's energy flows through you," he explained. "You can use it to create light, manipulate shadows, and sense other magical beings."

Amara listened intently, eager to try out her new skills. Lucas guided her through a series of exercises, starting with simple tasks like creating a small orb of light in her palm. At first, she struggled to focus the energy, but with patience and practice, she began to see progress.

"You're doing great," Lucas encouraged. "It takes time, but you're a natural."

As the days turned into weeks, Amara's confidence grew. She spent her mornings training with Lucas and the other Guardians, and her afternoons studying the history and lore of their order. She learned about past battles, legendary Guardians, and the ongoing struggle to keep the balance.

Outside of her training, Amara tried to maintain a semblance of her normal life. She went to school, hung out with her friends, and kept up with her homework. But it wasn't easy. The weight of her new responsibilities often left her feeling isolated, unable to share her secret with anyone.

One evening, after a particularly grueling training session, Amara sat on the porch of the cottage, staring up at the moon. She felt a presence beside her and looked up to see Lucas.

"Hey," he said, sitting down next to her. "You did well today. Don't be so hard on yourself."

Amara sighed. "It's just... a lot to take in. I feel like I'm living two lives."

Lucas nodded, understanding. "I know it's tough. But you're not alone. We're all here for you. And you're stronger than you think."

His words were comforting, and Amara felt a

flicker of hope. She knew the path ahead would be challenging, but with the support of her fellow Guardians, she believed she could rise to the occasion.

As the moon rose higher in the sky, casting its silvery light over the forest, Amara made a silent vow. She would embrace her destiny, honor her father's legacy, and become the Guardian she was meant to be.

Chapter 4

HIGH SCHOOL DRAMA

Balancing her new life as a Moon Guardian with the everyday challenges of high school proved to be more difficult than Amara had anticipated. Between training sessions and late-night study groups with the Guardians, she struggled to keep up with her schoolwork and maintain her friendships.

One morning, Amara rushed into Crescent Grove High School, barely making it to her first class on time. She slid into her seat, out of breath, just as the bell rang. Her best friend, Jenna, shot her a concerned look from across the room.

"Are you okay?" Jenna whispered as the teacher began the lesson.

"Yeah, just a rough morning," Amara replied, forcing a smile. She hated lying to Jenna, but she couldn't risk revealing her secret.

At lunch, Amara joined Jenna and their other friends at their usual table. The conversation was lively, but Amara found it hard to focus. Her mind kept drifting back to her training and the new responsibilities that weighed heavily on her shoulders.

"Amara, are you even listening?" Jenna's voice broke through her thoughts.

"Sorry, what were you saying?" Amara asked, trying to appear engaged.

"I was just talking about the new student," Jenna said, her eyes twinkling with curiosity. "He transferred here last week. Have you met him yet?"

Amara shook her head. "No, I haven't. What's he like?"

"He's a bit mysterious," Jenna said with a grin. "But really cute. His name is Ryan, I think."

Amara's curiosity was piqued. She had been so consumed with her new role as a Guardian that she hadn't noticed the arrival of a new student. She made a mental note to keep an eye out for him.

Later that day, as she was heading to her locker, Amara accidentally bumped into someone, causing her books to scatter across the floor.

"I'm so sorry," she exclaimed, kneeling to pick up her things.

"It's okay," a voice said, and she looked up to see a tall boy with dark hair and striking green eyes. He smiled warmly, handing her one of her books. "I'm Ryan, by the way."

"Amara," she replied, feeling a slight blush creep up her cheeks. "Nice to meet you."

Ryan seemed friendly enough, but there was something about him that made Amara feel both intrigued and cautious. She couldn't shake the feeling that there was more to him than met the eye.

Chapter 5

THE MYSTERIOUS NEW STUDENT

Over the next few days, Amara found herself crossing paths with Ryan more frequently. They had several classes together, and he often sat near her, striking up conversations. Despite her initial reservations, she began to enjoy his company. He was charming, intelligent, and had a way of making her laugh even when she felt overwhelmed.

One afternoon, as they were leaving school, Ryan caught up with Amara. "Hey, do you want to grab a coffee or something? I could use a break from studying."

Amara hesitated. She had a training session with Lucas later, but she was also curious about Ryan and eager to learn more about him. "Sure," she said finally. "Why not?"

They walked to a nearby café and found a cozy corner to sit in. As they sipped their drinks, Ryan asked, "So, how are you finding Crescent Grove?"

"It's a nice place," Amara replied. "I've lived here my whole life, so it's home."

Ryan nodded thoughtfully. "Must be nice to have that sense of stability. I've moved around a lot."

"Why's that?" Amara asked, intrigued.

"My dad's job," Ryan said with a shrug. "We never stay in one place for too long."

Amara sensed there was more to the story, but she didn't press him. Instead, she asked about his interests and hobbies, and they chatted easily for the next hour. She found herself drawn to him, but there was still that nagging feeling that he was hiding something.

As they left the café, Ryan turned to her and said, "You know, Amara, there's something different about you. I can't quite put my finger on it, but you're... special."

Amara's heart skipped a beat. Did he know about her powers? She forced a laugh. "I'm just an ordinary girl, Ryan."

He smiled, but his eyes held a knowing look. "Maybe. But I think there's more to you than meets the eye."

As they parted ways, Amara couldn't shake the feeling that Ryan was right. There was more to her than met the eye – and maybe, just maybe, there was more to him too.

Chapter 6

FRIENDSHIP TENSIONS

The next few weeks were a blur of school, training, and increasingly complicated emotions. Amara's friendship with Ryan deepened, but it also created tensions with Jenna and her other friends. They noticed her growing closeness to Ryan and her frequent absences from their usual hangouts.

One afternoon, as Amara was packing up her books, Jenna confronted her. "Amara, can we talk?"

"Sure," Amara said, sensing the seriousness in her friend's tone.

They walked to a quiet corner of the schoolyard. Jenna crossed her arms, looking frustrated.

"You've been really distant lately. What's going on?"

Amara sighed. She wished she could tell Jenna everything, but she knew it wasn't safe. "I've just had a lot on my plate," she said evasively. "Family stuff, you know?"

Jenna's expression softened slightly, but she still looked hurt. "I get that, but I miss hanging out with you. And what's the deal with Ryan? You guys seem really close."

Amara bit her lip. "Ryan's just a friend. He's new here, and I guess I've been trying to help him settle in."

Jenna frowned. "It feels like you're shutting me out, Amara. We've always been honest with each other."

The guilt weighed heavily on Amara. She hated lying to Jenna, but she couldn't risk her friend's safety by revealing the truth. "I'm not trying to shut you out, Jenna. I promise. Things are just... complicated right now."

Jenna sighed. "Okay, I get it. Just... don't forget about us, okay? We care about you."

"I won't," Amara said, hugging her friend. "I promise."

As Jenna walked away, Amara felt a pang of sadness. She hoped that one day, she could tell Jenna everything. But for now, she had to keep her secrets, no matter how much it hurt.

Chapter 7

FIRST BATTLE

As the days grew shorter and the nights longer, Amara felt the tension in the air increase. The Guardians had warned her that a significant threat was on the horizon, and she could sense the dark forces growing stronger.

One evening, during a particularly intense training session, Selene called the Guardians together. "We have received reports of shadow creatures attacking a nearby village," she announced. "This will be Amara's first real battle. Lucas, you will accompany her."

Amara's heart raced. She had trained for this moment, but the reality of facing a true threat was daunting. Lucas placed a reassuring hand on her shoulder. "You'll do fine. Just remember your training."

As night fell, Amara and Lucas set out for the village. The air was thick with anticipation, and Amara felt the weight of her responsibilities pressing down on her. When they arrived, the scene was chaotic. Shadowy figures moved through the streets, causing fear and destruction wherever they went.

Lucas turned to Amara. "Focus on the light within you. Use it to dispel the darkness."

Nodding, Amara took a deep breath and summoned her powers. She created an orb of light in her hand, feeling its warmth and strength. With Lucas by her side, she moved through the village, using her light to drive back the shadow creatures.

The battle was fierce. The shadow creatures were relentless, but Amara's determination grew with each confrontation. She realized that the pendant's power was more potent than she had imagined, and with each pulse of light, she felt her confidence grow.

At one point, she found herself separated from Lucas. A particularly large shadow creature lunged at her, and for a moment, fear threatened to overwhelm her. But she remembered her training and the support of her fellow Guardians. Summoning all her strength, she created a blinding flash of light, disintegrating the creature into nothingness.

Breathing heavily, she looked around and saw Lucas fighting off the remaining creatures. With renewed vigor, she joined him, and together they managed to drive the shadows away. The village was safe, for now.

After the battle, the villagers thanked them, and Amara felt a deep sense of pride and accomplishment. Lucas smiled at her. "You did it, Amara. I'm proud of you."

As they made their way back to the cottage,

Amara felt a new level of respect for the Guardians' mission. She knew the road ahead would be filled with challenges, but she was ready to face them head-on.

Chapter 8

TRAINING AND TRIALS

The victory in the village was a significant milestone for Amara, but it was only the beginning. Selene and the other Guardians intensified her training, pushing her to explore the full extent of her powers.

Each day brought new challenges. Amara learned to create barriers of light to protect herself and others, to manipulate shadows to her advantage, and to sense the presence of dark forces from afar. Lucas was a patient and encouraging mentor, always there to guide her through her struggles.

One afternoon, during a particularly grueling session, Amara found herself growing frustrated. She was trying to control multiple light orbs at once, but they kept flickering out of existence. "I can't do it," she muttered, feeling defeated.

"Yes, you can," Lucas said firmly. "You're stronger than you think. Don't let doubt cloud your mind."

Taking a deep breath, Amara closed her eyes and focused. She imagined the light as an extension of herself, a part of her very being. Slowly, she felt the energy flow through her, steady and unwavering. When she opened her eyes, she saw the orbs glowing brightly, hovering in the air around her.

"That's it," Lucas said, a proud smile on his face. "You've got it."

Amara beamed with pride. She was beginning to understand that her powers were not just about strength but also about control and belief in herself.

As the weeks passed, Amara's bond with Lucas

deepened. They spent hours together, not just training, but also talking about their lives, hopes, and fears. Lucas confided in her about his own struggles when he first became a Guardian, and Amara found comfort in knowing she was not alone in her journey.

One evening, as they sat by a campfire after a long day of training, Amara looked at Lucas and said, "Thank you for believing in me. I don't know what I would do without you."

Lucas smiled warmly. "We're a team, Amara. We look out for each other. And you're going to be an incredible Guardian."

Chapter 9

UNCOVERING SECRETS

Despite her progress, Amara couldn't shake the feeling that there were still many mysteries about her powers and her father's legacy that she didn't fully understand. One night, after a particularly vivid dream about her father, she decided to confront Selene.

"Selene," she said, entering the elder Guardian's study. "I need to know more about my father and our family's connection to the Moon Guardians."

Selene looked up from her ancient texts, her expression thoughtful. "Your father was a remarkable Guardian, Amara. He had a deep understanding of the moon's power and a strong connection to our order. But there are things about his past that even I do not fully know."

Amara felt a pang of frustration. "There has to be something. Anything that can help me understand my powers better."

Selene sighed and stood up, leading Amara to a hidden chamber beneath the cottage. Inside, there were relics and artifacts from past Guardians, including a journal that belonged to her father. "This is your father's journal," Selene said, handing it to Amara. "Perhaps it will provide the answers you seek."

Taking the journal, Amara felt a surge of emotion. She thanked Selene and returned to her room, eager to read the words her father had written. As she pored over the pages, she discovered a wealth of knowledge about the Moon Guardians, their history, and their powers. Her father's entries were filled with insights, experiences, and even personal thoughts and feelings.

One entry in particular caught her attention. It

spoke of a hidden power, a rare ability that only a few Guardians possessed. This power, known as the "Lunar Heart," allowed a Guardian to channel the moon's energy in ways that could alter the very fabric of reality.

Amara's heart raced as she read the description. Could she possess this rare power? And if so, what did it mean for her future as a Guardian?

Determined to find out, Amara decided to speak to Selene again, this time with more specific questions. She needed to understand the full extent of her abilities and the role she was destined to play in the ongoing battle between light and dark.

Chapter 10

GROWING CLOSER

The more Amara learned about her powers, the more she realized how important it was to have allies she could trust. Her friendship with Ryan continued to deepen, and she found herself opening up to him in ways she hadn't with anyone else.

One afternoon, after school, Ryan invited Amara to join him for a walk in the park. As they strolled along the winding paths, they talked about everything and nothing, enjoying each other's company.

"You know, Amara," Ryan said, glancing at her with a serious expression. "There's something I've been meaning to tell you."

Amara's heart skipped a beat. "What is it?"

Ryan hesitated, then took a deep breath. "I haven't been completely honest with you. There's a reason I moved to Crescent Grove, and it's not just because of my dad's job."

Amara's mind raced. Could Ryan be connected to the supernatural world as well? "What do you mean?"

"I come from a family with a long history of... unusual abilities," Ryan said carefully. "We've been moving around because my dad has been trying to keep us safe from people who want to use our powers for their own purposes."

Amara's eyes widened. "So, you have powers too?"

Ryan nodded. "Yes, but they're different from yours. My family has a connection to the sun's energy, and I've been training to control it. When I met you, I sensed something special about you. That's why I wanted to get to know you better."

Amara felt a mix of relief and excitement. "I had a feeling there was more to you. I'm glad you told me."

Ryan smiled, a hint of vulnerability in his eyes. "I trust you, Amara. And I want to help you with whatever you're facing. We're stronger together."

As they continued their walk, Amara felt a newfound sense of hope. She wasn't alone in her journey, and with Ryan by her side, she believed they could face whatever challenges lay ahead.

Chapter 11

THE DARK THREAT

With Ryan now aware of Amara's secret and revealing his own powers, their bond grew even stronger. Together, they trained, blending their abilities of the moon and sun, creating new ways to combat the dark forces. It felt like everything was falling into place, but a storm was brewing just over the horizon.

One evening, during a particularly intense training session with Lucas, Selene burst into the clearing, her face etched with worry. "We've received troubling news," she announced. "A powerful dark force is gathering, stronger than anything we've faced before."

Amara and Lucas exchanged worried glances. "What do we know about it?" Amara asked.

Selene took a deep breath. "It's an ancient entity,

known as the Shadow King. He's been dormant for centuries, but now he's awakening. His power is immense, and he seeks to plunge the world into eternal darkness."

The gravity of the situation hit Amara like a tidal wave. She had faced shadow creatures before, but this was something entirely different. "What can we do?"

"We must prepare," Selene said firmly. "And we need all the help we can get. Amara, you and Ryan must continue to train together. Your combined powers may be our only hope."

As the days passed, the Guardians worked tirelessly to strengthen their defenses and prepare for the impending battle. Amara and Ryan's training intensified, pushing them to their limits. The more they trained, the more they discovered new ways to merge their abilities, creating powerful light and energy attacks that could potentially counter the Shadow King's darkness.

Despite the looming threat, Amara found solace in her growing relationship with Ryan. They spent their nights under the stars, talking about their hopes and fears, finding comfort in each other's presence. Ryan's optimism and unwavering support gave Amara the strength she needed to face the challenges ahead.

One night, as they sat together on the rooftop of Amara's house, Ryan turned to her and said, "No matter what happens, we'll face it together. We're stronger when we're united."

Amara nodded, feeling a deep sense of gratitude. "Thank you, Ryan. I don't know what I'd do without you."

Chapter 12

BETRAYAL AND TRUST

As the day of the confrontation with the Shadow King drew closer, tensions ran high among the Guardians. Everyone was on edge, knowing that the battle could determine the fate of their world.

One evening, while Amara was reviewing battle strategies with Selene and Lucas, they were interrupted by a frantic knock on the door. It was Jenna, her face pale and eyes wide with fear.

"Amara, I need to talk to you," Jenna said urgently. "It's about Ryan."

Amara's heart sank. "What is it?"

Jenna took a deep breath, glancing nervously at Selene and Lucas. "I overheard something... something about Ryan. He's been in contact with someone from the dark forces. I think he might be betraying us."

Amara's mind reeled. She trusted Ryan with her life, but Jenna's words planted a seed of doubt. "Are you sure?"

"I heard him talking on the phone, mentioning the Shadow King," Jenna insisted. "Please, Amara, you have to be careful."

Conflicted, Amara decided to confront Ryan. She found him in the clearing where they usually trained, his expression lighting up when he saw her. But the warmth in his eyes faded when he saw the look on her face.

"Ryan, we need to talk," Amara said, her voice trembling.

"What's wrong?" Ryan asked, concern evident in his voice.

"Jenna told me she overheard you talking about

the Shadow King," Amara said, searching his eyes for any sign of deceit. "She thinks you're betraying us."

Ryan's expression hardened. "Amara, you have to believe me. I would never betray you. I did talk to someone, but it was to gather information, to help us prepare for the battle."

Amara wanted to believe him, but the doubt lingered. "Why didn't you tell me?"

"I didn't want to worry you," Ryan said, stepping closer. "Everything I've done has been to protect you, to protect us."

Tears welled in Amara's eyes. "I don't know what to think. This battle is too important, and I can't afford to take any chances."

Ryan took her hands in his, his grip firm but gentle. "Amara, look at me. We've trained together, fought together. You know me. Trust me."

After a moment of intense silence, Amara nodded, her resolve strengthening. "Okay. I trust you, Ryan. But you have to promise me, no more secrets."

Ryan nodded, relief washing over his face. "I promise. We'll face this together, just like we always have."

Chapter 13

THE LUNAR ECLIPSE

The night of the lunar eclipse arrived, and with it, the battle against the Shadow King. The Guardians gathered in the forest clearing, their faces determined but tinged with fear. The air was thick with tension, the sky darkening as the moon began to wane.

Amara stood at the center, her pendant glowing brightly. Ryan stood beside her, his own power radiating warmth. Selene and Lucas were on either side, ready to lead the charge.

As the eclipse reached its peak, the Shadow King emerged from the darkness, a towering figure cloaked in shadow. His presence was suffocating, the air around him crackling with dark energy.

"Guardians," he hissed, his voice echoing

through the clearing. "You are too late. The darkness will consume all."

Amara felt a surge of fear but pushed it down, focusing on the light within her. "We won't let that happen," she said, her voice steady.

The battle erupted with a fury. The Guardians fought valiantly, their powers clashing with the Shadow King's dark energy. Amara and Ryan worked in perfect harmony, their combined abilities creating powerful bursts of light that drove back the shadows.

Despite their efforts, the Shadow King was relentless. He seemed to grow stronger with each passing moment, feeding off the fear and despair in the air. Amara felt her strength waning, but she refused to give up.

"Amara, we have to combine our powers," Ryan said, his voice strained. "It's the only way."

Nodding, Amara took Ryan's hand, focusing all

her energy on their shared light. Together, they created a blinding beam of pure energy, aimed directly at the Shadow King. The dark figure screamed in rage as the light engulfed him, the shadows around him dissipating.

For a moment, it seemed like they had won. But the Shadow King wasn't defeated yet. With a final, desperate attack, he sent a wave of darkness crashing towards them. Amara felt the cold, suffocating force envelop her, threatening to drag her into oblivion.

"Amara!" Ryan's voice broke through the darkness, his grip on her hand tightening. "Stay with me!"

Drawing on the last reserves of her strength, Amara focused on the light within her, pushing back against the darkness. With a final, powerful burst, the light exploded outward, banishing the Shadow King once and for all.

The clearing fell silent, the air clear and still. The Guardians stood, breathless and exhausted, but victorious. The moon shone brightly in the sky, a symbol of their triumph.

Chapter 14

AFTERMATH

In the days following the battle, Crescent Grove slowly returned to normal. The villagers celebrated the Guardians' victory, grateful for their protection. Amara and Ryan were hailed as heroes, their bond stronger than ever.

Amara spent time reflecting on everything that had happened. She had faced her fears, uncovered her true potential, and protected those she loved. But she knew the journey was far from over. There would always be new threats, new challenges to face.

One evening, as she sat with Selene and Lucas, Amara asked, "What happens now?"

Selene smiled, her eyes twinkling with pride. "Now, we continue to train, to prepare for whatever comes next. You have proven yourself to be a true Guardian, Amara. The future is yours to shape."

Amara nodded, feeling a sense of peace. She looked at Lucas, who had been her mentor and friend through it all. "Thank you for everything," she said softly.

Lucas grinned. "You're a natural, Amara. I'm proud of you."

Chapter 15

A NEW BEGINNING

With the threat of the Shadow King behind them, Amara embraced her role as a Moon Guardian with renewed determination. She continued to train, honing her powers and learning new ways to protect the balance between light and dark.

Her relationship with Ryan blossomed, their bond growing deeper with each passing day. They faced their challenges together, supporting each other through thick and thin.

One evening, as they watched the sunset from their favorite spot in the forest, Ryan turned to Amara and said, "I have something for you."

He handed her a small, intricately carved box. Inside was a pendant, similar to her own, but in the shape of a sun. "This is a symbol of our unity," Ryan said, his eyes shining with love.

"Together, we can face anything."

Amara felt tears of joy in her eyes as she took the pendant and put it around her neck. "Thank you, Ryan. I love it."

As the sun dipped below the horizon, casting the world in a warm, golden glow, Amara felt a deep sense of contentment. She was ready to face whatever the future held, knowing she had the strength, the support, and the love she needed to succeed.

The adventure was far from over, but Amara was ready for whatever came next. She was a Guardian, and her story was just beginning.

EPILOGUE

The moon hung low in the sky, casting a silvery glow over the tranquil town of Crescent Grove. The battle against the Shadow King had left its mark on the town and its inhabitants, but the Guardians' victory brought a renewed sense of peace and hope. Amara stood on the rooftop of her house, looking out over the quiet streets, reflecting on the events that had changed her life forever.

With the Shadow King defeated, the immediate threat had passed, but Amara knew that their world was still fraught with danger. As a Moon Guardian, she had a responsibility to protect the balance between light and dark. The journey had only just begun, and the challenges ahead would test her in ways she could scarcely imagine.

Ryan joined her on the rooftop, his presence a comforting reminder of their shared purpose.

"The town seems so peaceful now," he remarked, gazing at the moonlit landscape.

Amara nodded. "For now, yes. But I can't shake the feeling that something else is coming. The Shadow King was just one part of a much larger darkness."

Ryan turned to her, his expression serious. "We'll be ready. Whatever comes next, we'll face it together."

Amara smiled, drawing strength from his unwavering support. "Thank you, Ryan. I couldn't do this without you."

As they stood together, a shooting star streaked across the sky, a reminder of the infinite possibilities and challenges that lay ahead. Amara felt a sense of determination settle within her. She was ready to embrace her destiny, to face whatever trials awaited her and the Guardians.

Back at the cottage, Selene and Lucas were discussing the recent events and planning their next steps. Selene looked up as Amara and Ryan entered. "There is much we need to prepare for," she said, her tone grave. "The Shadow King's defeat has stirred other dark forces. We must stay vigilant."

Lucas nodded in agreement. "We've received reports of strange occurrences in other parts of the world. It seems the darkness is spreading."

Amara felt a chill run down her spine. "What do we do?"

"We strengthen our defenses, continue our training, and seek out new allies," Selene replied. "There are others like us, Guardians of different realms, who can help us in this fight."

Ryan stepped forward, his resolve clear. "We'll do whatever it takes to protect our world."

As they gathered to discuss their plans, Amara

couldn't help but feel a sense of anticipation. The battle against the Shadow King had been just the beginning. There were greater threats to face, new mysteries to unravel, and powerful allies to discover.

The moon cast its light over them, a symbol of hope and guidance. Amara knew that their journey would be long and arduous, but she was ready. Together with her friends and fellow Guardians, she would face the coming darkness and protect the balance between light and dark.

As the night deepened, the Guardians made their preparations, ready to confront whatever challenges awaited them. And in the distance, beyond the horizon, a new dawn was breaking, heralding the beginning of their next adventure.

To be continued in "Eclipsed Realms: Solar Flares"

ABOUT THE AUTHOR

Luna Arwen has always been captivated by the moonlit nights and the whisper of ancient legends carried on the wind. Growing up in a quaint town surrounded by dense forests, she spent her childhood exploring nature and weaving fantastical tales inspired by the world around her. Her love for storytelling was nurtured by a deep fascination with the mystical and the supernatural, which eventually led her to pen the enchanting "Eclipsed Realms" series.

Luna's journey as a writer began with the simple joy of creating worlds where magic and reality intertwine. Her debut novel, "Lunar Shadows," has captivated readers with its blend of suspense, magic, and heartfelt emotion. The story of Amara Matthews, a seemingly ordinary girl destined to become a powerful Moon Guardian, has resonated with young readers who find themselves transported into a realm where light and darkness battle for supremacy.

When Luna isn't lost in her world of words, she enjoys stargazing, exploring hidden trails, and spending time with her beloved cat, Misty, who often serves as her writing companion. Her passion for the supernatural and her deep connection to nature continue to inspire her stories, each one a journey into the unknown.

Luna Arwen invites you to join her on this magical adventure and discover the wonders and dangers of the "Eclipsed Realms." She hopes that her books will ignite your imagination, stir your emotions, and remind you of the endless possibilities that lie within the pages of a good story.

DISCOVER MORE BY LUNA ARWEN

If you enjoyed "Lunar Shadows," Luna encourages you to explore the next thrilling installment in the "Eclipsed Realms" series, "Solar Flares." Follow Amara and her friends as they face new challenges, uncover deeper secrets, and continue their battle to protect the balance between light and dark.

Stay connected with Luna Arwen through her website and social media for updates on upcoming releases, exclusive content, and behind-the-scenes glimpses into her writing process. Luna loves hearing from her readers and cherishes the community of book lovers who share her passion for the mystical and the magical.

Thank you for being a part of this journey. The adventure is just beginning, and Luna can't wait to share more stories with you.

ACKNOWLEDGMENTS

First and foremost, my heartfelt gratitude goes to my sister, Elizabeth. Your love, encouragement, and unwavering belief in me have been the cornerstone of my journey. Wherever you are, I hope you feel the depth of my appreciation and love. This book is a tribute to the magic and strength you have always brought into my life.

To my parents, who fostered my love for stories and supported my every dream. Your endless patience and guidance have shaped me into the person I am today. Thank you for always believing in the power of imagination.

A special thank you to my close friends who have stood by me through thick and thin. Your late-night conversations, endless enthusiasm, and honest feedback have been invaluable. You've celebrated every milestone and helped me navigate every challenge. I couldn't have done this without you.

To my beta readers and critique partners, your insights and perspectives have been instrumental in shaping "Lunar Shadows." Thank you for your time, your keen eyes, and your honest opinions. Your contributions have made this story stronger and richer.

To my editor, whose expertise and guidance turned my rough manuscript into a polished novel. Your dedication and attention to detail have been incredible. Thank you for helping me find the heart of this story and bringing it to life.

To my publisher, who saw potential in my words and gave me the opportunity to share my story with the world. Your support and belief in "Lunar Shadows" have made this dream a reality.

To my readers, thank you for embarking on this journey with me. Your enthusiasm and love for these characters mean the world to me. Each of you has a special place in my heart. Your support and encouragement drive me to keep writing and exploring new realms.

And finally, to the mystical nights and moonlit skies that inspired this tale. Thank you for reminding me that magic exists all around us, if only we choose to see it.

With endless gratitude,

Luna Arwen